D1647768

HISTORY SPEAKS
PICTURE BOOKS PLUS READER'S THEATER

Alice Ray and THE SALEM WITCH TRIALS

BY **SHANNON KNUDSEN**

ILLUSTRATED BY **RUTH PALMER**

M MILLBROOK PRESS / MINNEAPOLIS

For Eliot and Felicity —RP

Publisher's note: Just as we use Miss or Mrs. with a woman's last name, Puritans in the late 1600s called a woman Goody or Goodwife. They called a man Goodman. They used "Mister" for important officials.

Text copyright © 2011 by Shannon Knudsen
Illustrations © 2011 by Lerner Publishing Group, Inc.

All rights reserved. International copyright secured. No part of this book may be reproduced, stored in a retrieval system, or transmitted in any form or by any means—electronic, mechanical, photocopying, recording, or otherwise—without the prior written permission of Lerner Publishing Group, Inc., except for the inclusion of brief quotations in an acknowledged review.

Millbrook Press
A division of Lerner Publishing Group, Inc.
241 First Avenue North
Minneapolis, MN 55401 U.S.A.

Website address: www.lernerbooks.com

The image in this book is used with the permission of: © Maurice Savage/ Alamy, p. 33.

Library of Congress Cataloging-in-Publication Data

Knudsen, Shannon, 1971–
    Alice Ray and the Salem witch trials / by Shannon Knudsen ; illustrated by Ruth Palmer.
        p.   cm. — (History speaks: picture books plus reader's theater)
    Includes bibliographical references.
    ISBN 978–0–7613–5879–4 (lib. bdg. : alk. paper)
    1. Trials (Witchcraft)—Massachusetts—Salem—History—17th century—Juvenile literature. I. Palmer, Ruth, ill. II. Title.
KFM2478.8.W5K68 2011
812'.6—dc22   2010027426

Manufactured in the United States of America
1 – CG – 12/31/10

CONTENTS

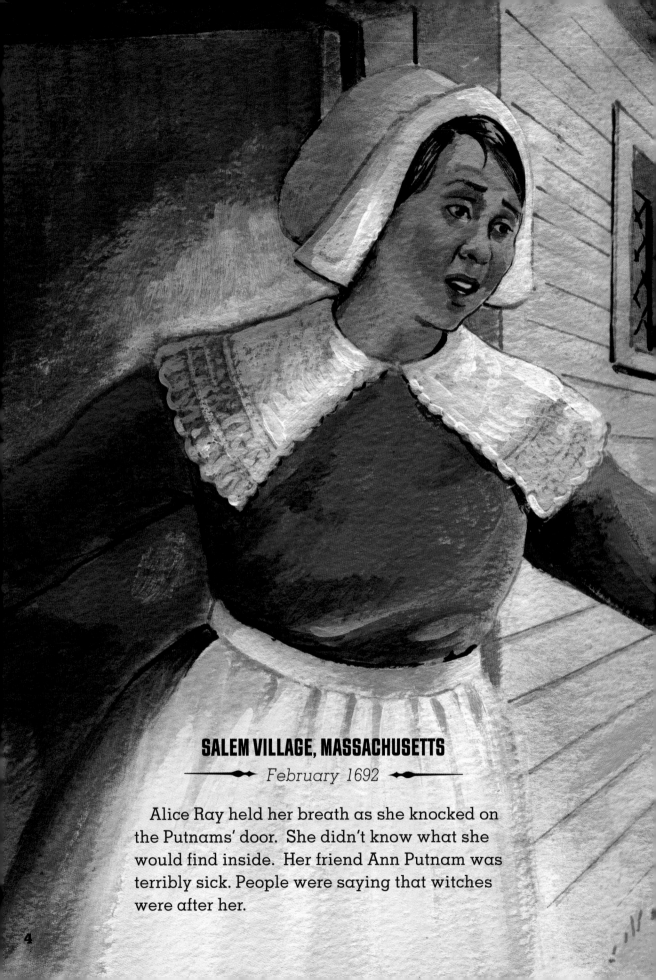

SALEM VILLAGE, MASSACHUSETTS

◆ February 1692 ◆

Alice Ray held her breath as she knocked on the Putnams' door. She didn't know what she would find inside. Her friend Ann Putnam was terribly sick. People were saying that witches were after her.

Alice had never seen a witch. But she had heard that witches didn't serve God, as all good Puritans did. Good Puritans of Salem lived by strict moral rules. But witches served the devil. In return, the devil gave them magic powers. People said that's why witches could move as spirits, without being seen. They could also make you sick. They could kill your cattle or horses. Worst of all, they could cause you terrible pain until you agreed to become a witch too.

Ann's mother let Alice in. "Please come inside," she told Alice. "God willing, it will do Ann good to see a friend."

Ann did not look well. Her breathing sounded strange, like dry branches in the wind. When she saw Alice, her eyes grew wide.

"Have you brought them with you?" she asked.

Alice was confused. "Brought who?"

"The ones who hurt me. Goody Osborne and Goody Good. Oh!" Ann lurched upward from her bed. "They are here! Choking me! Make them stop!" Her head tossed wildly from side to side.

Goodwife Putnam tried to calm her
daughter. "Shhh," she whispered.
"It's Alice Ray come to comfort you,
Ann. Just Alice. No other."

Alice thought her ears must be tricking her. Goodwife Sarah Osborne was quite old. She was so sick that she could hardly leave her bed. How could she be a witch?

And Goodwife Sarah Good? It was true that almost no one liked her. She and her husband were so poor that she had to beg for food. If you gave her something, she might snap at you as she took it. And if you gave nothing, she muttered strangely.

But Alice didn't mind Sarah Good. She had a kind heart once you got to know her. And she was so sweet to her little girl, Dorcas.

No, Sarah Good couldn't be a witch.

Alice sat beside her friend and took her hands.
"I will pray for you," she promised.
    "Thank you," Ann said. Then she gasped.
"Get away from me, Sarah Good!" she cried.

Alice had to say something. "I know Sarah Good," she told Ann. "She wouldn't hurt anyone. Could it be someone else who harms you, Ann?"

It was the wrong thing to say. Ann started to breathe very quickly. "Water," she gasped. Her mother ran to fetch it.

Suddenly, Ann seemed normal again. She looked straight into Alice's eyes. "The only reason you would say such a thing," she hissed, "is if you are a witch yourself!"

"Oh!" Alice cried. "No, no. I am not!"

Goody Putnam came in with a cup and held it to Ann's lips. "I think you had best go, Alice," she said. "I fear Ann is very ill today."

Alice hurried home. Did Ann really think she might be a witch? Was she truly sick at all? Alice had no idea.

Over the next few days, three more Puritan girls called Sarah Good a witch. She was arrested. Nearly the whole village came to the meetinghouse on the day she was questioned.

John Hathorne, an important Puritan official, began. "Sarah Good, what evil spirit helped you harm these children?"

"None," she said.

"Have you made a contract with the devil?"

"No."

"Why do you hurt these children?"

"I do not hurt them."

Mr. Hathorne called the four sick girls to come to the front of the room. The moment they faced Sarah Good, all four began to scream.

"No! No!" shouted Elizabeth Hubbard.

"She pinches me!" cried Betty Parris.

"Oh, it hurts!" said Ann Putnam.

"Stop her!" screamed Abigail Williams. She fell to the floor. Her whole body shook.

"Why do you lie to us?" Mr. Hathorne shouted at Sarah. "Why do you torment these poor children?"

"I do not hurt them!" Sarah said. "I am no witch."

"Why have you not come to meeting for more than a year?" It was a terrible thing to miss meeting. Almost everyone came twice a week, to pray and give praise to God.

Sarah glared at Mr. Hathorne. "I am poor. I have no clothes fit to wear to meeting."

The questions went on and on. Finally, Mr. Hathorne turned toward the crowd. "Will anyone defend this woman?"

Alice wanted to speak up. But Ann Putnam was staring at her. If Alice said anything kind about Sarah Good, Ann would hate her for it. She might even say that Alice was a witch.

Alice found herself on her feet. She ran from the meetinghouse as fast as she could go.

Sarah was taken to a prison near Salem. Several weeks later, Uncle Samuel came home with terrible news.

"Those poor sick girls have named Dorcas Good as a witch."

Aunt Mary gasped. "She's a child! Not more than four or five years old!"

Uncle Samuel nodded. "There is more. Dorcas has confessed. And she said her mother is a witch too."

"She's too little to understand what she says!" Alice cried. "That may be," Uncle Samuel said. "But she is being sent to prison in Boston, where Goodwife Good is now being held."

"What will happen to them?" Alice asked.

"A trial, I expect. All we can do is pray for them. And wait."

The waiting went on for weeks. So did the wailing of the sick girls. They named more and more villagers as witches.

Alice tried to go about her days like normal. She helped Aunt Mary cook and clean. She made candles and soap and scrubbed clothes.

She studied her lessons and practiced reading the Bible. She went to the meetinghouse for worship every Sunday and Thursday. And she prayed.

Nothing was normal, though. In June, Sarah Good was brought to Salem for her trial. Alice had never seen a person look so tired or so thin.

The trial began with the same questions Sarah had been asked before. Sarah again said she was innocent. And as before, the sick girls moaned and screamed that Sarah was hurting them.

Witnesses told stories about Sarah. One man said she had made his cows sick after an argument. A woman claimed her baby boy got a rash after she refused to give Sarah a meal.

It took only a few minutes for the judges to declare Sarah Good guilty of witchcraft. Next, they would decide what her punishment would be.

One of the judges spoke to the crowd. "The law says that a witch must be put to death. Does anyone wish to defend Sarah Good from this sentence?"

Alice stood up. Her legs were shaking.

"I will," she said. Her voice was just a whisper. But she tried again, and this time, the whole room heard her. "I will speak!"

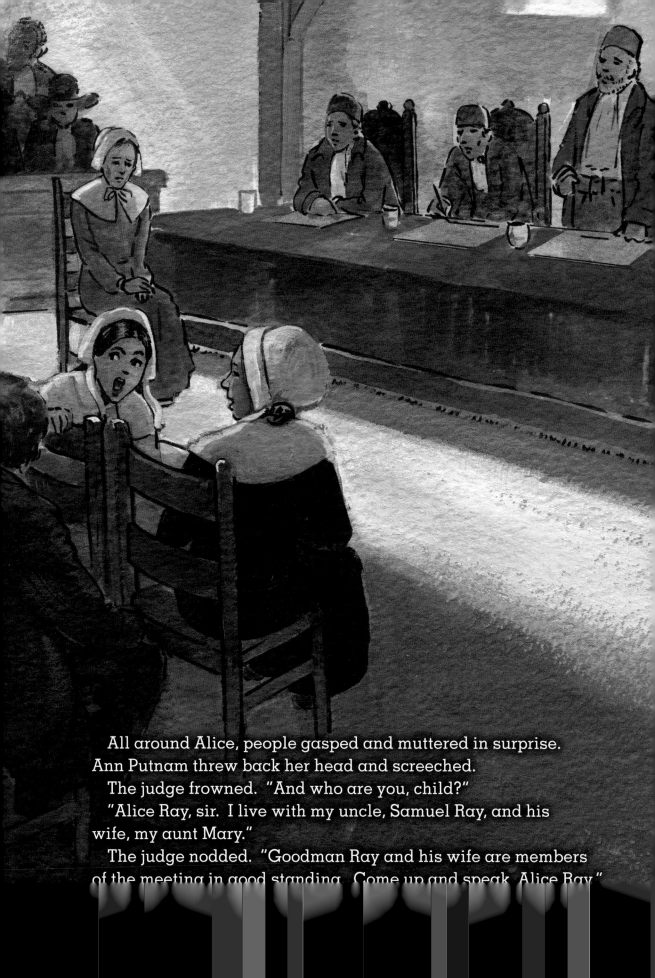

All around Alice, people gasped and muttered in surprise. Ann Putnam threw back her head and screeched.

The judge frowned. "And who are you, child?"

"Alice Ray, sir. I live with my uncle, Samuel Ray, and his wife, my aunt Mary."

The judge nodded. "Goodman Ray and his wife are members of the meeting in good standing. Come up and speak, Alice Ray."

Before she began, Alice looked straight at Ann Putnam and the other sick girls.

"I am very sorry for your suffering," she said. "I pray for you all."

Ann stopped moaning. Alice went on. "Sarah Good is poor, and her life has been hard. But I have never seen her harm anyone. She is a wonderful mother."

Alice turned to look at Sarah. "I should have spoken up sooner. I am very sorry I did not. I do not think Goodwife Good could be a witch. And she should not have to die."

"Thank you, Alice Ray. You may go," the judge said.

Alice left the court with head high and her heart full of hope for a miracle. But no miracle came. Sarah Good and four other women were hanged in July.

Alice cried when Aunt Mary told her the news. "It isn't fair," she said. "I wish I could have helped her."

Aunt Mary stroked her hair. "You did help her. You spoke up for her."

Alice sniffled.

"Sometimes," Aunt Mary said, "all we can do is look for ways to make something good out of evil."

Alice hugged her aunt.

The next day, Alice went to see
William Good, Sarah's husband.
She told him how sorry she
was about Sarah.

William just looked at
the ground.

"My aunt and uncle
sent me to ask you to
supper tonight. You
and Dorcas," Alice said.

William snorted.
"Now that would take
some witchcraft
indeed."

"What do you mean?"
Alice asked.

"To free Dorcas from the Boston jail," he explained.

Alice couldn't believe it. Dorcas had not been brought back to Salem with her mother! The little girl was trapped alone in a dark, smelly prison, far from home.

"They have her in chains," William went on. Alice saw tears in his eyes.

"Will the jailer not let her go free?" she asked.

The question brought another snort from William. "Surely! For fifty pounds."

Fifty pounds! Alice had never seen so much money. William Good could work for years and still not earn fifty pounds.

She didn't know what to say. But William Good had already turned away from her.

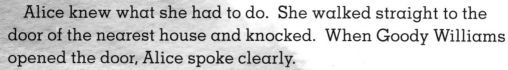

Alice knew what she had to do. She walked straight to the door of the nearest house and knocked. When Goody Williams opened the door, Alice spoke clearly.

"Good morning, Goodwife. Could you spare a few pennies for a little girl in prison? We must pay the jailer to bring Dorcas Good home to her father."

Goody Williams was silent. Alice wondered if the request had angered her. But after a moment, Goody Williams gave a small nod and stepped into the house. She returned with a few coins and quickly dropped them into Alice's hand. With another nod, she turned back inside.

Alice stopped at three other houses that day. She visited more each day in the weeks after. Uncle Samuel saved some coins for Alice each week too. Months later, Alice and her uncle had collected nearly enough to pay the bail. Alice smiled. Dorcas Good would be home by Christmas. It had taken a long time, but Alice Ray made all the good she could out of the evil that the witch trials had brought to Salem in 1692.

Alice Ray was not a real person. But Sarah Good was. She was hanged for witchcraft in Salem Village in July 1692. Her daughter, Dorcas, was also a real person. When she was four or five years old, she was accused of witchcraft. She spent nine months in prison. Dorcas wasn't freed until Samuel Ray paid fifty pounds for her bail in December 1692. In modern money, that would be many thousands of dollars.

We don't know why Samuel Ray paid that money. And we actually don't know how he raised it. But we know a little bit about what happened to Dorcas. Those months in prison changed her. She had been healthy, but after her time in prison, her mind and body were broken. She could not take care of herself, even when she grew up. Her father, William Good, had to pay for a helper to care for her.

In modern times, people don't often believe in witches. But to the people of Salem, nothing was more important than religion. And their religion taught that witches were real. The people of Salem believed that the devil wanted people to disobey God. And they believed that people who agreed to serve the devil were given magic powers. Women with these powers were called witches. When people had bad luck or got sick, they sometimes thought that witches had caused their trouble.

Why did Ann Putnam and the other girls claim to be attacked by witches? They may have been pretending. They probably enjoyed the attention they got. Some of them may have believed they were truly being hurt. Maybe they were in

THE SALEM WITCH TRIALS MEMORIAL, SALEM, MASSACHUSETTS. EACH BENCH BEARS THE NAME OF AN ACCUSED WITCH WHO WAS PUT TO DEATH.

pain because of an illness of some kind.

Sarah Good was one of the first people the girls accused. No one ever saw her or anyone else hurt the girls. But people believed that witches could move as spirits without being seen. When the girls claimed that the spirit of Sarah Good was hurting them, she couldn't prove that she wasn't. Neither could the other people who were accused. The people of Salem thought that the worst kind of evil had come to their village.

The ministers and judges who ran the trials changed their minds in late 1692. They decided that no one should be found guilty of witchcraft based on spirit sightings alone. That meant that the sick girls could not prove who was hurting them. The trials ended in May 1693. By then, more than 150 people had been accused and arrested. Fourteen women and five men had been hanged. Several people, including Sarah Osborne, died in prison. One man died from torture during his questioning.

Many years later, Ann Putnam apologized for her part in the trials. She said that the devil had tricked her into accusing innocent people. Some of the judges and ministers who took part in the trials apologized too. In 1712, the government gave money to the family members of many of the people who were hanged. One of them was William Good, who was paid thirty pounds for his family's suffering.

Performing Reader's Theater

Dear Student,

Reader's Theater is a dramatic reading. It is a little like a play, but you don't need to memorize your lines. Here are some tips that will help you do your best in a Reader's Theater performance.

BEFORE THE PERFORMANCE

- **Choose your part:** Your teacher may assign parts, or you may be allowed to choose your own part. The character you play does not need to be the same age as you. A boy can play the part of a girl, and a girl can play the part of a boy. That's why it's called acting!

- **Find your lines:** Your character's name is always the same color. The name at the bottom of each page tells you which character has the first line on the next page. If you are allowed to write on your script, highlight your lines. If you cannot write on the script, you may want to use sticky flags to mark your lines.

- **Check pronunciations of words:** If your character's lines include any words you aren't sure how to pronounce, check the pronunciation guide on page 45. If a word isn't there or you still aren't sure how to say it, check a dictionary or ask a teacher, librarian, or other adult.

- **Use your emotions:** Think about how your character feels in the story. If you imagine how your character feels, the audience will hear the emotion in your voice.

- **Use your imagination:** Think about how your character's voice might sound. For example, an old man's voice will sound different from a baby's voice. If you do change your voice, make sure the audience can still understand the words you are saying.

- **Practice your lines:** Even though you do not need to memorize your lines, you should still be comfortable reading them. Read your lines aloud often so they flow smoothly.

DURING THE PERFORMANCE

- **Keep your script away from your face but high enough to read:** If you cover your face with your script, you block your voice from the audience. If you have your script too low, you need to tip your head down farther to read it and the audience won't be able to hear you.

- **Use eye contact:** Good Reader's Theater performers look at the audience as much as they look at their scripts. If you look down, the sound of your voice goes down to the script and not out to the audience.

- **Speak clearly:** Make sure you are loud enough. Say all your words carefully. Be sure not to read too quickly. Remember, if you feel nervous, you may start to speak faster than usual.

- **Use facial expressions and gestures:** Your facial expressions and gestures (hand movements) help the audience know how your character is feeling. If your character is happy, smile. If your character is angry, cross your arms and be sure not to smile.

- **Have fun:** It's okay if you feel nervous. If you make a mistake, just try to relax and keep going. Reader's Theater is meant to be fun for the actors and the audience!

Cast of Characters

NARRATOR 1

NARRATOR 2

NARRATOR 3

READER 1:
Goodwife Putnam, Sarah Good, Aunt Mary

READER 2:
John Hathorne, Judge, William Good

ANN PUTNAM

ALICE RAY

UNCLE SAMUEL

ALL:
Everyone except sound

SOUND:
This part has no lines. The person in this role
is in charge of the sound effects.
Find the sound effects for this script
at www.lerneresource.com.

The Script

NARRATOR 1: Alice Ray lived in Salem, Massachusetts. Alice had a friend named Ann Putnam. In February of 1692, Ann was terribly sick. Alice went to visit her friend.

NARRATOR 2: People were saying that witches were after Ann. Alice had never seen a witch. But she had heard that witches served the devil. In return, the devil gave them magic powers. People said that witches could move without being seen.

NARRATOR 3: Witches could also make you sick. They could cause you terrible pain until you agreed to become a witch too.

SOUND: [knock on door]

NARRATOR 1: Alice held her breath at the Putnam's door. She didn't know what she would find inside. Ann's mother greeted her.

READER 1 (as Goodwife Putnam): Please come inside. God willing, it will do Ann good to see a friend.

NARRATOR 2: Ann did not look well. When she saw Alice, her eyes grew wide.

ANN: Have you brought them with you?

ALICE: Brought who?

ANN: The ones who hurt me. Goody Osborne and Goody Good. They are here! Choking me!

Next Page — **NARRATOR 3**

NARRATOR 3: Ann lurched upward from her bed. Her head tossed from side to side. Goodwife Putnam tried to calm her daughter.

READER 1 (as Goodwife Putnam): Shhh. It's just Alice Ray come to comfort you, Ann.

NARRATOR 1: Alice couldn't believe it. Goodwife Sarah Osborne was quite old. She could hardly leave her bed. How could she be a witch?

NARRATOR 2: And Goodwife Sarah Good? Almost no one liked her. She and her husband were so poor that she had to beg for food. If you gave her something, she might snap at you as she took it. And if you gave nothing, she muttered strangely.

NARRATOR 3: But Alice didn't mind Sarah. Sarah had a kind heart once you got to know her. And she was sweet to her little girl, Dorcas.

NARRATOR 1: Alice sat beside her friend and took her hands.

ALICE: I will pray for you.

ANN: Thank you.

NARRATOR 2: Then Ann gasped.

ANN: Get away from me, Sarah Good!

NARRATOR 2: Alice had to say something.

ALICE: Sarah Good wouldn't hurt anyone. Could it be someone else who harms you, Ann?

Next Page — **NARRATOR 3**

NARRATOR 3: It was the wrong thing to say. Ann started to breathe very quickly. She cried for water. Her mother ran to fetch it. Suddenly, Ann seemed normal again. She looked into Alice's eyes.

ANN: You would only say such a thing if you are a witch yourself!

ALICE: No, no. I am not!

NARRATOR 1: Goody Putnam came in with a cup and held it to Ann's lips.

READER 1 (as Goodwife Putnam): You had best go, Alice. I fear Ann is very ill today.

NARRATOR 2: Alice hurried home.

ALICE: Does Ann really think I might be a witch? Is she truly sick at all?

NARRATOR 3: Over the next few days, three more girls called Sarah Good a witch. She was arrested. Nearly the whole village came to the meetinghouse on the day she was questioned.

SOUND: [crowd murmuring]

NARRATOR 1: John Hathorne, a Puritan official, began to question Sarah Good.

READER 2 (as Hathorne): What evil spirit helped you harm these children?

READER 1 (as Sarah Good): None.

Next Page — **READER 2**

READER 2 (as Hathorne): Have you made a contract with the devil?

READER 1 (as Sarah Good): No.

NARRATOR 2: Mr. Hathorne called the sick girls to come to the front of the room. The moment they faced Sarah Good, all four began to scream.

SOUND: [girls screaming]

NARRATOR 3: The girls cried out in pain. One begged Hathorne to stop Sarah Good. The girl's whole body shook.

READER 2 (as Hathorne): Why do you torment these poor children, Sarah Good?

READER 1 (as Sarah Good): I do not hurt them! I am no witch.

READER 2 (as Hathorne): Why have you not come to meeting for more than a year?

NARRATOR 1: It was a terrible thing to miss meeting. Almost everyone came twice a week, to pray.

READER 1 (as Sarah Good): I am poor. I have no clothes fit to wear to meeting.

NARRATOR 2: Mr. Hathorne turned toward the crowd.

READER 2 (as Hathorne): Will anyone defend this woman?

NARRATOR 3: Alice wanted to speak up. But if Alice said anything kind about Sarah Good, Ann Putnam would hate her for it. She might even say that Alice was a witch. Alice ran from the meetinghouse as fast as she could go.

Next Page — **SOUND**

SOUND: [running]

NARRATOR 1: Sarah went to prison. Weeks later, Uncle Samuel came home with terrible news for Alice and her aunt Mary.

UNCLE SAMUEL: Those poor sick girls have named Dorcas Good as a witch.

READER 1 (as Aunt Mary): She's a child! Not more than five years old!

UNCLE SAMUEL: There is more. Dorcas has confessed. And she said her mother is a witch too.

ALICE: She's too little to understand what she says!

UNCLE SAMUEL: That may be. But she is being sent to prison in Boston, where Goodwife Good is being held. All we can do is pray for them. And wait.

NARRATOR 2: The waiting went on for weeks. So did the wailing of the sick girls. They named more and more villagers as witches.

NARRATOR 3: Alice tried to go about her days like normal. She helped Aunt Mary cook and clean. She made candles. She went to the meetinghouse every Sunday and Thursday. And she prayed.

NARRATOR 1: Nothing was normal, though. In June, Sarah Good was brought to Salem for her trial. Alice had never seen a person look so tired or so thin.

NARRATOR 2: The trial began with the same questions as before. Sarah again said she was innocent. The sick girls again screamed that Sarah was hurting them.

Next Page — **SOUND**

SOUND: [girls screaming]

NARRATOR 3: Witnesses told stories about Sarah. One man said she had made his cows sick after an argument. A woman claimed her baby got a rash after she refused to give Sarah food.

NARRATOR 1: It took only a few minutes for the judges to declare Sarah Good guilty of witchcraft. Next, they would decide what her punishment would be. A judge spoke to the crowd.

READER 2 (as judge): The law says that a witch must be put to death. Does anyone wish to defend Sarah Good from this sentence?

NARRATOR 2: Alice stood up. Her legs shook.

ALICE: I will.

NARRATOR 3: Her voice was just a whisper. But she tried again. This time, the whole room heard her.

ALICE: I will speak!

SOUND: [gasps from crowd]

NARRATOR 1: All around Alice, people gasped in surprise. Ann Putnam threw back her head and screeched.

READER 2 (as judge): And who are you, child?

ALICE: Alice Ray, sir. I live with my uncle, Samuel Ray, and his wife, my aunt Mary.

READER 2 (as judge): Goodman Ray and his wife are members of the meeting in good standing. Come up and speak, Alice Ray.

Next Page — **NARRATOR 2**

NARRATOR 2: Before she began, Alice looked straight at Ann Putnam and the other sick girls.

ALICE: I am very sorry for your suffering. I pray for you all.

NARRATOR 3: Ann stopped moaning. Alice went on.

ALICE: Sarah Good is poor. Her life has been hard. But I have never seen her harm anyone. She is a wonderful mother.

NARRATOR 1: Alice turned to look at Sarah.

ALICE: I should have spoken sooner. I am very sorry I did not. I do not think Goodwife Good could be a witch. And she should not have to die.

READER 2 (as Judge): Thank you, Alice Ray. You may go.

NARRATOR 2: Alice left the court with her heart full of hope for a miracle. But no miracle came. Sarah Good and four other women were hanged in July. Alice cried when Aunt Mary told her the news.

ALICE: It isn't fair. I wish I could have helped her.

READER 1 (as Aunt Mary): You did help her. You spoke up for her. Sometimes, all we can do is look for ways to make something good out of evil.

NARRATOR 3: Alice hugged her aunt. The next day, Alice went to see William Good, Sarah's husband. She told him how sorry she was about Sarah. William just looked at the ground.

ALICE: My aunt and uncle sent me to ask you to supper tonight. You and Dorcas.

Next Page — **READER 2**

READER 2 (as William): That would take some witchcraft indeed.

ALICE: What do you mean?

READER 2 (as William): To free Dorcas from the Boston jail.

NARRATOR 1: Alice couldn't believe it. Dorcas had not been brought back to Salem with her mother! The little girl was alone in a dark prison, far from home.

ALICE: Will the jailer not let her go free?

READER 2 (as William): Surely! For fifty pounds.

NARRATOR 3: William Good could work for years and still not earn fifty pounds. Alice didn't know what to say. But William Good had already turned away from her.

NARRATOR 1: Alice knew what she had to do. She walked straight to the door of the nearest house and knocked. When Goody Williams opened the door, Alice spoke clearly.

ALICE: Good morning, Goodwife. Could you spare a few pennies for a little girl in prison? We must pay the jailer to bring Dorcas Good home to her father.

NARRATOR 2: For months, Alice and Uncle Samuel worked to collect enough money. Their efforts would bring Dorcas home by Christmas.

NARRATOR 3: It would take a long time, but Alice Ray would make all the good she could out of the evil that the witch trials had brought to Salem.

ALL: The End

Pronunciation Guide

Dorcas: DOHR-kuss
Goody: GU-dee
Salem: SAY-luhm

Glossary

Goodman: a title of respect for a man, like "Mister" in modern times. Men were also called "Mister," as in "Mr. Hathorne," if they had an important job or lots of money.

Goodwife: a title of respect for a married woman, like "Ms." or "Mrs." in modern times. Women whose husbands were called "Mister" were called "Mistress" instead of Goodwife.

Goody: short for *goodwife*

meeting: a worship service that lasted several hours

meetinghouse: a place where members of a church met to worship

pound: a unit of money in England and its colonies. In Salem in 1692, a woman could earn a pound in about a month as a servant.

witch: a woman who people thought had magical powers and served the devil. A male witch was called a wizard or a warlock.

Selected Bibliography

Boyer, Paul, and Stephen Nissenbaum, eds. *Salem-Village Witchcraft: A Documentary Record of Local Conflict in Colonial New England.* Boston: Northeastern University Press, 1993.

Gragg, Larry. *The Salem Witch Crisis.* New York: Praeger Publishers, 1992.

Marten, James, ed. *Children in Colonial America.* New York: New York University Press, 2007.

Roach, Marilynne K. *The Salem Witch Trials: A Day-by-Day Chronicle of a Community Under Siege.* New York: Cooper Square Press, 2002.

Further Reading and Websites

BOOKS

Aller, Susan Bivin. *Anne Hutchinson.* Minneapolis: Lerner Publications Company, 2010.
Read about another woman put on trial in Massachusetts in the 1600s—not for witchcraft but for preaching.

Kerns, Ann. *Wizards and Witches.* Minneapolis: Lerner Publications Company, 2010.
Discover witches and wizards in world folklore, myth, and folk culture as well as European history and modern entertainment.

Pipe, Jim. *You Wouldn't Want to Be a Salem Witch.* New York: Franklin Watts, 2009.
Learn what it was like to be a Salem witch in this illustrated adventure.

Warner, John. *Massachusetts*. Minneapolis: Lerner Publications Company, 2002.
Find out more about the history of Massachusetts as well as modern life there.

Yolen, Jane, and Heidi Elisabet Yolen Stemple. *The Salem Witch Trials: An Unsolved Mystery from History.* New York: Simon and Schuster, 2004.
Readers are invited to become history detectives and try to puzzle out what happened in Salem in 1692.

Zumbusch, Amelie von. *The True Story of the Salem Witch Hunts.* New York: PowerKids Press, 2009.
This brief introduction provides basic information about the witch hunts.

WEBSITES

Salem Witch Trials Documentary Archive and Transcription Project
http://www.salemwitchtrials.org
View historical maps of Salem Village, read documents from the trials, and learn about the people involved.

Salem Witch Trials—Learning Adventures
http://school.discoveryeducation.com/schooladventures/salemwitchtrials/
Read about the lives of children in Salem in 1692, and find out more about the real Sarah Good, including her final words.

Secrets of the Dead: The Witches' Curse
http://www.pbs.org/wnet/secrets/previous_seasons/case_salem/index.html
Some researchers believe that a fungus played a major part in the witch trials. Find out why at this PBS site.

Dear Teachers and Librarians,

Congratulations on bringing Reader's Theater to your students! Reader's Theater is an excellent way for your students to develop their reading fluency. Phrasing and inflection, two important reading skills, are at the heart of Reader's Theater. Students also develop public speaking skills such as volume, pacing, and facial expression.

The traditional format of Reader's Theater is very simple. There really is no right or wrong way to do it. By following these few tips, you and your students will be ready to explore the world of Reader's Theater.

EQUIPMENT

Location: A theater or gymnasium is a fine place for a Reader's Theater performance, but staging the performance in the classroom works well too.

Scripts: Each reader will need a copy of the script. Scripts that are individually printed should be bound into binders that allow the readers to turn the pages easily. Printable scripts for all the books in this series are available at www.lerneresource.com.

Music Stands: Music stands are very helpful for the readers to set their scripts on.

Costumes: Traditional Reader's Theater does not use costumes. Dressing uniformly, such as all wearing the same color shirt, will give a group a polished look. Specific costume pieces can be used when a reader is performing multiple roles. They help the audience follow the story.

Props: Props are optional. If necessary, readers may mime or gesture to convey objects that are important to the story. Props can be used much like a costume piece to identify different characters performed by one reader. Prop suggestions for each story are available at www.lerneresource.com.

Background and Sound Effects: These aren't essential, but they can add to the fun of Reader's Theater. Customized backgrounds for each story in this series and sound effects corresponding to the scripts are available at www.lerneresource.com. You will need a screen or electronic whiteboard for the background. You will need a computer with speakers to play the sound effects.

PERFORMANCE

Staging: Readers usually face the audience in a straight line or a semicircle. If the readers are using music stands, the stands should be raised chest high. A stand should not block a reader's mouth or face, but it should allow for the reader to read without looking down too much. The main character is usually placed in the center. The narrator is on the end. In the case of multiple narrators, place one narrator on each end.

Reading: Reader's Theater scripts do not need to be memorized. However, the readers should be familiar enough with the script to maintain a fair amount of eye contact with the audience. Encourage readers to act with their voices by reading with inflection and emotion.

Blocking (stage movement): For traditional Reader's Theater, there are no blocking cues to follow. You may want to have the students turn the pages simultaneously. Some groups prefer that readers sit or turn their back to the audience when their characters are "offstage" or have left a scene. Some groups will have their readers move about the stage, script in hand, to interact with the other readers. The choice is up to you.

Overture and Curtain Call: Before the performance, a member of the group should announce the title and the author of the piece. At the end of the performance, all readers step in front of their music stands, stand in a line, grasp hands, and bow in unison.

Please visit www.lerneresource.com for printable scripts, prop suggestions, sound effects, a background image that can be projected on a screen or electronic whiteboard, a Reader's Theater teacher's guide, and reading-level information for all roles.